Amanda at Bat

Amanda at Bat

Lisa K. Winkler

ILLUSTRATED BY
Stella Sormani

Book design by Solveig Bang

To Lydia

(L.K.W.)

To Lauren

(S.S.)

At the first T-ball game of the season, Coach Cooper announced: "Batting order today is alphabetical by last names, A to Z."

Amanda Zimmerman practiced swinging her bat. What if the bases were loaded? Maybe she'd hit the ball and bring everyone home.

All those with A to V last names took their turns.

Suddenly, the second graders arrived for their game.

"We have to stop," said Coach Cooper. "Barbie Velasquez, you're last for today."

When her three older brothers met her after their baseball practice, they showed Amanda no sympathy.

"Don't be a baby. Be tough. That's what being an athlete is," they said.

At the next game,
Coach Cooper announced:
"Tallest to shortest today, kids."

The shortest, Amanda, would be last.
With only five kids before her,
it would soon be her turn.

Suddenly, the sky darkened,
roared with thunder and
crackled with lightening.
Heavy rain fell, forming huge
puddles on the field.

"We have to cancel,"
yelled Coach Cooper.
"It's too dangerous."

At dinner, Amanda tried
to look happy.

"Did you play today?" asked
her dad. Her mom told him
what had happened.

"Oh well, you'll get a chance
next time."

DECEMBER

S	M	T	W	TH	F	S
						1
2	3	4	5	6	7	8
9	10	11	12	13	14	15
16	17	18	19	20	21	22
23	24	25	26	27	28	29
30	31					

At the next game,
Coach Cooper changed the
batting order again.

"By birthdays today,
January to December."

Amanda's birthday was December
15th. She would be last at bat.
Would she play today?
All the kids born through
November had their turns.

Suddenly Coach Cooper's phone rang. "Oh, I can't believe it. I'll be right there."

His pregnant wife had to get to the hospital, two weeks early.

"We have to end the game."

"But, Coach, I'm next.
I haven't played yet.
Please, can we finish?"
Amanda begged, trying
hard not to cry.

"Sorry. You'll play next week."

And he left.

That night, Amanda complained.
"Why couldn't I be born
Zamanda Aimmerman?
Why wasn't I born in January?
And why am I so short?"

Her family shook their heads.

"Look, we can't help when you were
born, or your height, or your last
name. We can't make the sun shine or
prevent Coach's wife from having a
baby or keep the second graders off
the field. There's nothing you can do."

In bed, Amanda
lay awake, thinking.

At the next game the coach began:
"Today's batting order... "

"Wait!" shouted Amanda.

Coach Cooper bent to
listen to her.

When he stood up, he said:
"Wish I'd thought of those myself."

He announced: "Today's order,
reverse alphabet, Z to A.
The next game, shortest to tallest,
and the last game, December to
January birthdays.

Now play ball!"

So Amanda Zimmerman,
a short girl born in December,
grabbed her bat, and
headed to home plate.

THE END

FOR ADULTS

Reading *Amanda at Bat* to young children could stimulate discussions about fairness and how a young person can creatively solve problems. Here are some questions you could use to start this conversation:

1. Have you ever had a time when you felt things weren't fair? What did you do about it?

2. Can you think of any other ideas to help Amanda solve her problem?

3. What do you think of how her brothers responded to her complaints? Did you agree or disagree with them and why?

4. Amanda solved her problems by herself. Do you think it would have been better if she asked for help from her teammates or family?

ABOUT THE AUTHOR

Lisa K. Winkler is a writer and educator. She has a Masters in Education with a focus in children's literature. She writes plays, poetry and blogs, and loves to read, knit, cycle, cook, do yoga, and be a grandmother. www.lisakwinkler.com

ABOUT THE ILLUSTRATOR

Stella Sormani is an artist and art teacher. She also likes gardens, reading, and running with her friend Lisa Winkler, when their schedules allow. Her daughter, whose last name begins with an S, is petite and born in November.

Made in the USA
Middletown, DE
26 May 2016